DISNEY'S
THE EMPEROR'S
NEW GROOVE

The Junior Novelization

Adapted by Kathleen W. Zoehfeld

DISNEY PRESS

New York

Printed in the United States of America

First Edition
1 3 5 7 9 10 8 6 4 2

This book is set in 13-point Minion.

Library of Congress Catalog Card Number: 00-101748
ISBN: 0-7868-4429-9
For more Disney Press fun, visit www.disneybooks.com

Contents

Chapter 1

It's All about ME

Kuzco stood in his bedroom admiring himself in the mirror. "I'm really the coolest, most important guy in the world," he crooned. He flung his golden sun headdress high and cracked his knuckles confidently as the headdress twirled down, alighting perfectly on his royal head. He was only seventeen years old, but Kuzco was emperor of all he surveyed!

As he strode down the halls of his palace, servants rushed to roll out red carpets and open doors for him. Kuzco sighed importantly. He was ready to start his grueling day of cutting ribbons, christening ships, and kissing babies (with a pair of rubber lips, of course, since the idea of touching a baby revolted him).

After these exhausting royal duties, Kuzco posed on his throne with an air of boredom and demanded his servants fan him and bring him water.

He had only to snap his fingers, and his butler set out plates and cutlery. At another snap, a banquet appeared. Not satisfied with the food on *his* plate, Kuzco sat in the center of the banquet table and ordered his subjects to feed him the juiciest fruits from their own.

Stuffed with food and full of himself, Kuzco commanded his theme-song guy to sing his favorite song: "This perfect world begins and ends with . . ."

BOOM! He burst through a giant double doorway, flattening the guards on the other side.

". . . ME!" Kuzco strutted and danced as his subjects looked on. Oblivious, he moonwalked right into a tottering old man. The music screeched to a halt.

"Aaaaarrghh! You threw off my groove!" the emperor snarled.

"I'm sorry, but you've thrown off the emperor's groove," echoed a burly guard. And, without missing a beat, he tossed the old man out the window.

"*Sorrrrry!!!*" The old man's voice faded as he plummeted down the stone face of the palace.

"As you were saying," Kuzco said to his theme-song

guy with a smirk. He heard the words of his favorite song build back to a crescendo, and, with a leaping karate kick, he opened the door to the hall where he would perform his most challenging task of the day—choosing a bride for the most perfect, richest, most powerful ball of charisma the world had ever known: *himself.*

"HA! Boom baby!" he cried.

"Your Highness, it is time for you to choose your bride," said the nobleman in charge.

"All-righty, trot out the ladies. Let's take a look-see," said Kuzco.

The nobleman clapped his hands, and the most lovely women in the kingdom stepped in line for inspection.

Kuzco looked them over, unimpressed. "Is this really the best you can do?" he asked.

"Ohhh, yes . . . ohhh, no . . . I, I mean . . . perhaps . . ." the nobleman stammered.

"Hey!" Kuzco interrupted the nobleman's nervous babble. "Where's Yzma?"

"Sire, she's in the throne room. It's Ignore the Pleas of the Peasants Day," explained the nobleman.

"She's where?" cried Kuzco.

"Ummmm . . . she's in the throne room. Please don't sacrifice me," the nobleman pleaded.

"She's in my throne room again? That's *my* throne

room! It's not her throne room. It's mine! It's got my likeness carved on it, not hers. In my book that makes it mine, mine, mine . . . !" Kuzco ranted. He stormed off toward the throne room, with nervous servants bowing and flinging open the doors as he went.

Meanwhile, unaware of Kuzco's approach, his adviser, Yzma, was indeed perched on the throne. A spiky-haired, evil-eyed woman—scary beyond all reason—Yzma was enjoying the momentary power and a satisfying bit of cruelty.

She looked down with contempt at a peasant who was bowing before her. "And why have you come here today?"

"Well . . . I mean . . . Y-y-your Highness, Your Grace . . . I mean the reason I am here is about your taxes," stammered the peasant.

Yzma's personal assistant, Kronk, stood beside the throne, ready to make himself useful. A fly buzzed around Yzma's head, and Kronk swished his meaty hand in the air to shoo it away.

Soon the dim-witted Kronk had an even more difficult problem to figure out: the fly landed on *him*. He swatted it enthusiastically, knocking himself off balance and falling flat on his back in the process.

Yzma tried to ignore him. She was busy giving the

poor peasant a tongue-lashing. "It's no concern of mine whether your family has, what was it again?"

"Ummm . . . food," said the peasant.

"Ha! You really should have thought of that before you became peasants. We're through here! Take him away. Next!"

With that, the emperor appeared silently at her side.

"Gaagh!" gasped Yzma.

Kuzco smiled and waggled his fingers. "Hi, there."

Yzma sprang off the throne and dusted it with her scarf. "Oh, Your Highness. Uh, oh, uh, hee, hee, oh, oh," she stammered.

"You were doing it again," Kuzco pointed out.

"Doing what?" Yzma asked.

"Doing my job," said Kuzco. "I'm the emperor and you're the emperor's adviser. Remember that?"

"But, Your Highness . . ." Yzma said. "I was only dealing with meaningless . . ." As Yzma rattled on, Kuzco's eyes glazed over in boredom.

"Good thinking, Yzma. What do you say, Kuzco?" said Kronk, clapping his big, sporty hand on the emperor's shoulder.

"Whoa!" cried Kuzco. "No touchy. Nooo touchy. No touch."

The doors to the throne room opened and a servant

announced that the leader of the local village had arrived for his audience with the emperor.

"Oh great, send him in," said Kuzco. He turned and glared at Yzma. "Oh, and by the way, you're fired."

"Fired?" cried Yzma. "What, what—what do you mean, 'fired'?"

"How else can I say it? You're being let go; your department is being downsized; we're going in a different direction; we're not picking up your option—take your pick, I've got more."

"But, Your Highness, I have been nothing if not loyal to the empire for many, many years," sputtered Yzma.

"Hey, everyone hits their stride. You just hit yours fifty years ago," quipped Kuzco.

Humiliated, Yzma stormed away, growling and grinding her teeth in fury.

Chapter 2

The Emperor's New Home

O utside the throne room, Pacha rested his weary bulk on a bench and wiped his brow with his rough, woolen hat. It had been a long trip from the village, but Emperor Kuzco had demanded that he, the village leader, come to him immediately. Pacha worried and fretted, wondering what the emperor had on his mind.

The imposing throne room doors opened, and Pacha quietly entered the emperor's chamber.

"Afternoon, Your Highness. I'm here because I received a summons to—"

"Hey, there he is. My main village man," sang Kuzco.

"Um, Pacha. Anyway, I got this summons—"

"Pacha!" cried the emperor. "That's right, you are just the man I wanted to see!"

"I am?" said Pacha quizzically.

"Word on the street is you can fix my problem," said Kuzco.

Pacha looked doubtful.

"You *can* fix my problem, can't you?" cried Kuzco.

"Sure, I'll . . . do what I can," offered Pacha.

"Good, good. That's what I wanted to hear. Are you aware of just how important your village is to the empire?"

"Well," Pacha began, as Kuzco led him into the model room, "I know we grow the crops that you use here at the palace, and we also herd the llamas that you . . ."

Pacha stopped in midsentence, surprised. "My village?" he asked. There, right in front of him, was a miniature model of the beautiful green hillside and the village that was his home.

"Oh yeah, you've got a pretty sweet little setup there on top of that hill, don't you?" Kuzco chuckled.

"Yeah," agreed Pacha. "My family has lived on that hilltop for the last six generations."

"Uh-huh," said Kuzco, unimpressed. "So tell me, where do you find you get the most sun?"

"Oh, I'd say just on the other side of these trees," replied Pacha. "When the sun hits that ridge just right, these hills sing."

"Well, that settles it," said Kuzco.

"Really?"

"Yep. Problem's solved. Thanks for coming." Kuzco waved to dismiss the portly peasant.

"That's it? That's all you wanted me for?" Confused, Pacha turned to walk away. He scowled to himself, wondering why in heaven the emperor had called him all this way for a question about sunshine.

"I just needed an insider's opinion before I okayed the spot for my pool," Kuzco commented to the air.

Pacha spun around. "Huh? Your . . . pool?"

Kuzco picked up the model of the gaudy architectural monstrosity he had designed and, **KERPLUNK**, plopped it down on top of the model of Pacha's village. "Welcome to Kuzcotopia! My ultimate summer getaway, complete with water slide!"

"What?" cried Pacha. The emperor's enormous "summer home" covered his entire village!

"Isn't it great? It's my birthday gift to me," said Kuzco with a contented sigh. "I'm so happy."

"Uh . . . ah . . . but . . . I don't understand how this could happen," stammered Pacha.

"Well, let me clear it up for you. At my birthday celebration tomorrow, I give the word and your town will be destroyed to make way for this," Kuzco declared, pointing to his model of Kuzcotopia. "So if I were you I'd pick up some change-of-address forms on the way home."

"But, but . . . where will we live?" asked Pacha.

"Hmmm." Kuzco scratched his head in mock thought. "Don't know." He beamed smugly. "Don't care. How's that?"

"Ah, but wait, you can't . . ." Pacha tried to protest, but two huge guards aimed their spears at him and glowered.

Kuzco brought his face close to Pacha's and whispered, "When I give the word, your little town-thingy will be . . . bye-bye." Kuzco waggled his fingers at Pacha as the guards escorted him out of the throne room. "Bye-bye."

Chapter 3

Yzma's Revenge

In another part of the palace, Yzma was still fuming over being fired. She scowled and raised a mallet over her head like a rail driver swinging a sledgehammer. **SMASH!** she brought it down on Kuzco's head— a stone replica of his head, that is—and it shattered into a million pieces.

Ever the able assistant, Kronk promptly replaced the smashed bust with a new one.

Yzma paced the room, still fuming. "He can't get rid of me that easily! Who does that ungrateful little worm think he is?"

She wheeled back and glared at the new bust. **SMASH!** Her mallet came down once again. Kronk replaced the bust with yet another.

SMASH! Yzma worked out her fury on head after regal head until Kronk was standing in rubble up to his knees.

"How could he do this to me?" Yzma raved as she swung the mallet. "Why, I practically raised him!"

"Yeah," agreed Kronk stupidly. "You think he would've turned out better."

"Yeah, go figure," said Yzma with a sneer.

"Well, it's better you're taking out your anger on these things instead of the real Kuzco, huh?" said Kronk.

Yzma beamed at Kronk as if he had just said the brightest thing she had ever heard. She grabbed him by his collar. "That's it, Kronk! That's it! I'll get rid of Kuzco!"

Kronk looked puzzled. "The real Kuzco?" he asked.

"Of course, the real Kuzco!" Yzma smiled her scheming smile. "Don't you see? It's perfect! With him out of the way and no heir to the throne, I'll take over and rule the empire! It's brilliant!"

Kronk was having trouble keeping up with her. "How does that work with you being fired and all?"

"The only ones who know about that are the three of us—soon to be the TWO of us!" Yzma cackled with glee.

Kronk pondered worriedly. "I'm one of those two, right?"

"To the secret lab!" exclaimed Yzma, ignoring him.

They dashed down the corridor, searching for the lever that would open the secret door. Kronk located one.

"Pull the lever, Kronk!" cried Yzma.

Kronk pulled, and a trapdoor opened up under Yzma's feet. Down she fell like a bucket plummeting into a deep well. Kronk peered into the dark shaft and after a few seconds heard a distant splash. "Uh-oh." He cowered as Yzma stomped back into the room like a drowned rat, with a crocodile attached to her behind.

"Why do we even *have* that lever?" she asked as she swatted the crocodile away.

Kronk shrugged. Yzma shoved him out of the way and yanked down the second lever. Finally, the secret door slid open. Before their eyes sat a shiny, fancy roller-coaster car, ready to carry them down to Yzma's lab, deep under the palace.

"Please remain seated and keep your arms and legs in at all times," a voice said as the safety bar came down across their laps. They zoomed down the winding track.

"Wheeeee!" cried Yzma.

"Put your hands in the air!" shouted Kronk gleefully. The car rolled to a stop just outside Yzma's secret lab.

Yzma and Kronk leaped from the car and gave each other a high five.

Yzma scanned her shelves for the right potion, musing over her murderous plot. "Ahh, how shall I do it? I know! I'll turn him into a flea. A harmless little flea. And then I'll put that flea in a box. And then I'll put that box inside another box. And then I'll mail that box to myself. And when it arrives, I'll smash it with a hammer! It's brilliant!"

Delighted with her plan, she raised her arms in triumph. As she did, she knocked over a beaker of poison, and it spilled onto one of her plants. The plant gasped and sputtered and crumpled over like a water lily in a hot desert.

Yzma admired the poison's quick action. "Or," she reconsidered, "to save on postage, I'll just poison him with this!"

She shoved a vial into Kronk's hands. "Take it, Kronk. Feel the power!"

"Ohhh, I can feel it!" cried Kronk.

Outside, lightning flashed. Yzma's cackling laughter rang through the lab as she worked out her evil plan. She would invite Kuzco to an elegant dinner—a birthday party for the mighty, all-powerful emperor. She gloated, knowing that Kuzco was so self-centered, he would never suspect a thing. A dash of poison in his drink and **PFFT**—his eighteenth birthday would certainly be his last.

That evening, Kronk donned an apron and busied himself preparing spinach puffs in the palace kitchen.

Yzma stalked through the room without even glancing at the feast Kronk had been laboring over. "So, is everything ready for tonight?" she asked.

"Oh yeah," said Kronk, nodding enthusiastically. "I thought we'd start off with soup and a light salad and then see how we feel after that."

"Not the dinner!" snapped Yzma. "The—you know."

Kronk thought for a moment. "Oh, right, the poison. The poison for Kuzco. The poison chosen especially to kill Kuzco. Kuzco's poison. That poison?"

"Yes, that poison," Yzma said.

Kronk pulled the vial out of his pocket to show her. "Gotcha covered."

"Excellent." Yzma glowed. "A few drops in his drink—I'll propose a toast—and he will be dead before dessert."

"Which is a real shame, because it's going to be delicious," said Kronk as he leaned over to sample his creation.

"Boom bam, baby!" The door flew open. The mighty emperor himself had arrived! He checked out Kronk's cooking. "Let's get to the grub. I am one hungry king of the world." He paused to give Yzma a haughty glance. "So, no hard feelings about being let go?"

Yzma clenched her teeth and flashed him the phoniest, most flattering grin she could muster. "None whatsoever. Kronk, get the emperor a drink."

He gave Yzma a secret nod. "Drink. *Riiiight.*"

Kronk poured three glasses of wine and added a few dashes of poison to Kuzco's glass. Wisps of red vapor rose over it as he carried the tray of drinks into the dining room. He was about to hand the emperor his glass when Kuzco said he thought he smelled something burning.

"My spinach puffs!" cried Kronk in dismay. He set down his tray and rushed back to the kitchen.

Yzma glanced at the drinks nervously and forced a smile for the emperor.

"So . . . he seems nice," said Kuzco, making awkward conversation.

"He is," replied Yzma. She wondered what on earth was taking Kronk so long in that kitchen.

"He's what, in his late twenties?" asked Kuzco indifferently. He stretched back in his chair in total boredom.

Finally, Kronk reappeared with his spinach puffs. "Saved 'em!" he cried.

"That's great, good job, very good," said Yzma and Kuzco together, both relieved to be ending their aimless conversation.

"Watch it, they're hot," Kronk said as he proudly served his savory puffs.

"Kronk, the emperor needs his *drink*," Yzma reminded him.

Kronk looked down at the glasses of wine on his tray. Which one had he poisoned? In the flurry over the spinach puffs, he had completely forgotten. Quickly he whisked the tray away, emptied a vase and poured all three drinks in, mixed them up, and poured the wine into the glasses again. This way, he figured, he couldn't go wrong.

"Hey, Kronky, everything okay back there?" asked Kuzco, wondering what was taking so long.

"Oh, uh, the drinks were a bit on the cool . . . uh, warm side," Kronk improvised lamely as he set the drinks before them.

"A toast to the emperor! Long live Kuzco!" Yzma lifted her glass, about to take a sip.

Kronk coughed, desperately signaling Yzma not to drink. As Kuzco gulped his down and smacked his lips in satisfaction, Yzma emptied her glass into a nearby plant. Kronk kept his mouth closed, letting the wine dribble down his chin.

They stared at Kuzco. Why wasn't he dying? They glanced at each other. Kronk shrugged. Then suddenly Kuzco flopped face down into his spinach puffs.

"Finally," said Yzma with a sigh of relief. "Good work, Kronk."

"Oh, they're easy to make. I'll get you the recipe," Kronk said, thinking she meant the spinach puffs.

Yzma was trying to decide what to do with the emperor when all of a sudden Kuzco sprang bolt upright again like a jack-in-the-box. "Okay, what were we saying?" he asked.

Yzma stared at Kuzco in disbelief. Two long llama ears were growing where his human ears had been! "We . . . were just making a toast to your long ear . . . er, life and healthy rule," she stammered.

"Right. So what are *you* going to do now? I mean, you've been around here for a long time and it might be difficult for someone of your age, adjusting to the private sector. Because you're, let's face it, no spring chicken . . . and I mean that in the best possible way." Kuzco rattled on and on, oblivious to his strange transformation. He held up his empty glass, looking for a refill. "Hey, Kronk, can you top me off, pal?"

Yzma made a clobbering motion with a stalk of broccoli, signaling Kronk to knock him out.

Kronk looked confused. "More broccoli?" he asked her.

"Hit him on the head," she hissed under her breath.

Kronk raised the broccoli platter and clonked Kuzco on the head with it. Kuzco flopped back down into his spinach puffs. By this time Kuzco had sprouted a llama snout, llama eyes, and llama fur.

"A llama?" shouted Yzma. "He's supposed to be dead!"

Kronk looked puzzled. "Yeah. Weird."

Yzma grabbed the vial of poison from his pocket. "Let me see that!" She turned the vial in her hand and read the label. "This isn't poison! This is extract of llama!"

She boiled over with anger. "Grrrrrrrr!"

"You know, in my defense, your poisons all look alike. You might think about relabeling some of them," Kronk said.

If only she didn't need him to help her get rid of that miserable emperor, Yzma could have knocked Kronk in the head with the broccoli platter right then and there. "Take him out of town and finish the job!" she ordered.

Chapter 4

Kuzco Gets Dumped

Kronk stuffed the unconscious Kuzco-llama into a big red sack. Then he hoisted the load over his shoulder and snuck out the side door of the palace. He hummed nonchalantly, trying to avoid suspicion as he made his way down the street to the canal.

When he reached the water's edge he tossed the bag. It landed with a satisfying splash. "Mission accomplished!" he declared.

He strode away, feeling pretty good about his success. But the menacing roar of the waterfall downstream reached his ears, and something about that sound made him feel uneasy. He turned and watched the bag floating away. He pictured Kuzco plummeting over the huge falls. And then the voice of his angel conscience began talking in his ear. "You're not just gonna let him die like that, are you?"

His devil voice countered angrily, "Don't listen to that guy. He's trying to lead you down the path of righteousness. I'm gonna lead you down the path that rocks!"

"Oh, come off it!" cried his angel voice.

"You come off it," countered the devil.

Poor Kronk couldn't decide what to do. Save him. Let him die. Save him. Let him die. Kronk's angel and devil voices debated noisily in his ears while Kuzco floated down the canal.

Finally, Kronk couldn't take their bickering anymore. He addressed them as forcefully as he knew how: "Listen, you guys, you're confusing me, so . . . um . . . BEGONE!"

He turned his attention back to the llama in the bag, and without a moment to lose, he began to chase after it. He leaped through the air like an acrobat and snatched the bag just seconds before it went over the edge of the waterfall.

Kronk had no idea what to do next. If Yzma caught him with the bag still in hand, she'd clobber him. He slung the wet sack over his shoulder again and jogged up the street. He ran down a flight of stairs trying to think. "Come on Kronky, come on Kronky. What to do? What to do? What do we do with the body?"

For Kronk, thinking *and* watching where he was going at the same time was a bit more than he could handle. He didn't see the cat that was sleeping on one of the stairs. *"YEOW!"* the cat howled as Kronk tripped over her, sending his sack flying through the air.

"Ow, ah, oh, ee, ow," Kronk cried as he tumbled down and landed on his head.

The bag bounced down the steps and landed smack on the back of a peasant's cart.

Pacha, fresh from his visit with the emperor, had just finished picking up some supplies in one of the city shops and did not see the bag o'llama land on his cart. He picked up his reins and led his own llama, Misty, through the city, while in the cart behind them—knocked out cold and wrapped in a bag—rode the emperor.

Kronk looked up from his fall to see Pacha and Misty heading off with the heavy bundle. "Hey, uh, hey you . . . you with the cart! Stop!" he yelled. But Pacha and Misty were out of earshot.

"This is not good," Kronk mused. "Hope that doesn't come back to haunt me."

Far out of town, Pacha sighed heavily and steered Misty and his cart up the hillside toward home. His heart ached at the thought that this might be the last time he would ever see his beautiful village.

Chapter 5

Whole Llama
Shakin' Going On

In their little house on the hillside, Pacha's wife, Chicha, and their two children waited for him to return home from his long trip.

"Mom, Mom, I think I'm still growing!" cried Tipo. "Measure me again!"

Chicha crouched down next to her small son and helped him stand up straight against the doorframe. She made a mark over his head.

"Mom, you and I both know that it's impossible for him to have grown in the last five minutes, isn't it?" his older sister, Chaca, argued.

Chicha pointed at the mark on the doorframe and

opened her eyes wide in mock surprise. "Tipo, look how much you've grown!"

Chaca fell for it. "What? Tipo, get out of the way. It's my turn again. Measure me!"

Chicha was chuckling and measuring Chaca once again, when Tipo spied Pacha approaching.

"Dad's home!" he cried.

"Hey, come here!" called Pacha.

The two children flew out the door and climbed all over their dad, laughing and kissing him wildly.

"Dad, I ate a bug today," announced Tipo.

Pacha raised his eyebrows. "Oh, was Mom baking again?" He leaned close to Tipo's ear and whispered, "Don't tell her I said that."

"I heard that!" cried Chicha. She stood up slowly and put her hands under her round belly. Her new baby was due in just a few months. "Okay, everybody move aside. Lady with a baby coming through," she joked. She leaned over to give Pacha a kiss.

"Dad-Dad-Dad!" cried Tipo, pointing to the doorframe. "Look how big I am!"

"We were all measured today," explained Chicha.

"I'm going through a growth spurt," said Tipo. "I'm as big as you were when you were me."

Pacha smiled. "You sure are."

"That's not as impressive as my loose tooth—see?" said Chaca, vying for attention. She showed him how she could wiggle it with her breath.

"Okay, okay, you two," said Chicha. "Our deal was that you could stay up until Daddy came home. Now say good night."

The children looked up at Pacha with big doe eyes. "Dad, do we have to?"

"Oh, sure, you two can stay up," said Pacha. "We're just going to sit around and talk about how much we love each other. Right, honey?" he cooed at his wife.

"Eeeeew . . . good night!" the kids called over their shoulders as they ran off to bed.

Chicha laughed. "Hey, so what did the emperor want?" she asked.

Pacha could not bear to tell his wife the terrible news. "You know what . . . he couldn't see me," he said, stalling.

"Couldn't see you? Why not?" asked Chicha.

"I don't know," Pacha lied.

"Well, that's just rude!" cried Chicha.

"Well, he *is* the emperor. I'm sure he's busy," Pacha tried.

Chicha shook her fist at an imaginary emperor. "No,

no, no! Emperor or no emperor, it's called common courtesy! If that were me, I'd march right back there and demand to see him. And you know I would."

"Sweetie, sweetie," said Pacha. "Think of the baby."

"Pacha, I'm fine. This baby's not coming for a while. But even if it was, I'd give that guy a piece of my mind. That kind of behavior is just . . . just . . . grrrr . . ." Chicha was so angry she ran out of words. "I've got to go wash something."

As his wife attacked the pile of dirty dishes in the sink, Pacha just stood there looking longingly around his home.

"Pacha, are you okay?" Chicha asked.

"Oh, yeah," said Pacha. He sighed. "I'm just a little tired from the trip." He shuffled outside to empty his cart and put Misty in her pen. How was he going to tell his family that they would have to leave their home?

He unhitched Misty and reached to take the first of the supplies from his cart, when he noticed the strange red bag. It was moving! "Whoa!" cried Pacha.

Dazed and confused, Kuzco the llama poked his head out and looked around. "Ooooohhhh," he moaned.

Pacha stroked Kuzco's mane kindly. "Where'd you come from, little guy?"

"No touchy!" cried the cranky llama.

Pacha shrank back in fright. "Aaaahhh! Demon llama!" he cried.

"Where?" cried Kuzco. Then he spotted Misty. "Aaaaahhhh!" he screamed, thinking she must be the demon the peasant was referring to. He leaped to his feet and tried to run away. But he didn't realize he had llama legs now. His hooves stumbled and his legs tangled and he went tumbling headfirst into a nearby fence.

"Oooooh . . . my head." He groaned.

Pacha thought perhaps this talking demon llama was not so powerful after all. "Okay, demon llama, take it easy. I mean you no harm," he said soothingly.

"What are you talking about? Oh wait, I know you! You're that whiny peasant!" cried Kuzco.

Pacha thought he recognized that voice! "Emperor Kuzco?" he asked with a gasp.

"'Who did you think you were talking to?" asked Kuzco.

"How did . . . um . . . you don't *look* like the emperor," said Pacha.

"What do you mean, I don't *look* like the emperor?" asked Kuzco.

Pacha waved his hand in front of his face and motioned for Kuzco to do the same.

"What is this?" mocked Kuzco. "Some kind of little game you country-folk like to . . . ?" He stopped in midsentence and stared at his hand in disbelief. It was a hoof!

"It can't be . . ." He bent over the water trough to look at his reflection. "My face!" he cried. "My beautiful, beautiful face! I'm an ugly, stinky llama!"

"Okay, okay, whoa, what happened?" asked Pacha.

"I'm trying to figure that out, okay?" Kuzco said. "I can't remember. I can't remember anything. Wait a minute. I do remember you! I remember telling you that I was building my pool where your house was, and then you got mad at me . . ." A light dawned in Kuzco's eyes, and he pointed at Pacha accusingly. "And then you turned me into a llama!"

"What?" cried Pacha. "No, I did not!"

"Yes!" Kuzco shouted. "And then you kidnapped me!"

"Why would I kidnap a llama?"

"I have no idea. You're the criminal mastermind, not me."

Pacha could not have been more confused. "What?"

"Hmmm . . . you're right. That's giving you way too much credit. Okay, I have to get back to the palace.

Yzma's got that secret lab. I'll just snap my fingers and order her to change me back." Kuzco struck a kingly llama pose and glared at Pacha. "Hey, you," he ordered, "no time to waste. Let's go!"

Kuzco marched away, expecting Pacha to follow, but the stout peasant stood his ground.

"Hey, Tiny, I want out of this body. Wouldn't you? Now, let's go!" snapped Kuzco.

"Build your summer home somewhere else," Pacha declared.

"You want to run that by me again?" said Kuzco.

"I can't let you go back unless you change your mind and build your summer home somewhere else."

"I got a little secret for you." Kuzco motioned Pacha closer and shouted in his ear, "I DON'T MAKE DEALS WITH PEASANTS!"

"Then I guess I can't take you back," said Pacha firmly.

"Fine. I don't need you. I can find my own way back," declared Kuzco, turning away.

"I wouldn't recommend it. It's a little dangerous if you don't know the way," warned Pacha.

"Nice try, pal." Kuzco sashayed toward the jungle.

"No, really, I'm telling you, there are jaguars and snakes and quicksand."

"La-la-la . . ." Kuzco sang, ignoring him.

"I'm not kidding. Listen, you cannot go in there."

Kuzco kept on walking, straight toward the deep dark jungle.

"Aaaagh, fine! Go ahead!" cried Pacha in exasperation. "If there's no Kuzco, there's no Kuzcotopia! Takes care of *my* problem."

Pacha headed back to his house, but he could not help casting one last worried glance toward the stubborn emperor-llama as he disappeared into the underbrush.

Chapter 6

Bucky, the Wonder Squirrel

Kuzco puffed himself up bravely and strode through the forest, mocking all the peasant's warnings. "Scary jungle, right. Oh, a leaf. Oh, it might attack me. Oh, it's a scary tree. I'm afraid." He giggled.

As he walked he heard the cries of monkeys and birds up above him in the branches. Around him the jungle growth was getting thicker. "Please—never find my way?" He chuckled to himself. "I'm the emperor, and as such, I am born with an innate sense of direction." He paused. The jungle had closed in on him. It looked the same in every direction. "Okay. Where am I?"

ZZZZZOOM. A fly buzzed past him. Then,

THWACK, it was suddenly stopped in midflight—trapped in a spider's web. Kuzco watched aghast as the huge spider descended on the fly and started chomping it with his powerful jaws. The fly buzzed in agony. Kuzco gulped.

"Ah, okay, that was the freakiest thing I've ever seen," he said. He heard rustling in the bushes behind him. He turned. The leaves shook. He panicked! "Aaaaaaaaaaaa!!!"

A little fuzzy squirrel hopped out of the bushes and held up an acorn in his paws.

"Grrr. What do you want?" Kuzco snapped.

"Gu gu buga?" asked the squirrel, offering him the nut.

"Oh, for me? Why, I don't know what to say," said Kuzco with a sarcastic smile.

"Gu gu bu gu bi gu lee ho," babbled the squirrel.

Kuzco grabbed the acorn and flung it at the squirrel's head. "Hit the road, Bucky!"

"Ow gu gu argh," little Bucky said, wincing.

Kuzco stormed off and promptly toppled down a hill, landing on his face, right in the middle of a pack of sleeping jaguars.

Kuzco gasped and held his breath. Bucky moved to the ledge above him to get a better view. He held up a big red balloon and threatened to pop it with a pin and awaken the sleeping beasts. The squirrel smiled sweetly.

"N-N-N- . . . no . . . don't . . . break," begged Kuzco breathlessly.

Bucky stuck the pin in the balloon. *KABLAM!* The jaguars didn't stir.

"HA!" cried Kuzco, triumphant.

That did it. The entire pack raised their heads together and growled.

Kuzco scrambled to his feet and ran, with the jaguars hard at his heels. He glanced back in terror, and just as he did he slammed into a low-hanging limb, flipped over it, and landed, right on the back of one of the angry jaguars. It was all Kuzco could take. He began to cry like a baby.

The jaguars skidded to a stop and Kuzco flew forward. He tumbled to the edge of a cliff. Trapped between the hungry jaguars and the dangerous precipice, Kuzco whimpered, "You . . . killer jaguars . . . whoa."

Lucky for Kuzco, Pacha's worries about the emperor had gotten the better of him. He'd told his wife that he was taking up her wise suggestion and going back to see the emperor once again. Little did she know how close the emperor actually was.

As Pacha struggled along the jungle trail, he heard

Kuzco's cries. With a brave Tarzan yell, he swung in on a vine, parting the jaguars and scooping up Kuzco just in the nick of time. "Don't worry, Your Highness. I gotcha. You're safe now."

SWOOSH—their swift momentum wheeled them around and around the limb that the vine was attached to. Around and around and around they went, until they were both strapped tightly to it. Then, under the weight of the llama and the hefty peasant, the limb began to crack.

"Maybe I'm new to this whole rescuing thing," said Kuzco, "but this, to me, might be considered kind of a step backward. Wouldn't you say?"

"Oh, no, no, it's okay. This, this is all right—we can figure this out . . ."

CRRRACK. The branch was about to give way!

"I hate you," said Kuzco as they went down.

Still strapped together on the limb, they bounced down a hillside and splashed into a roaring river.

"You call this a rescue?" sputtered Kuzco.

"Yeah, well, I don't see you coming up with any better ideas," Pacha replied.

"Well, if I did, you can be sure it wouldn't involve tying us to a tree!" cried Kuzco.

SPLASH, CRASH, BASH—their bickering stopped

as they twirled through the rapids, banging into the rocks left and right. They reached a calm place in the river and managed to crane their heads up for a look around. They had no idea where they were, but just downstream they could hear the ominous roar of a waterfall.

Kuzco coughed up some water. "I don't know about you, but I'm getting all funned out."

"Uh-oh," Pacha said with a groan.

"Don't tell me. We're about to go over a huge waterfall," Kuzco predicted wryly.

"Yep."

"Sharp rocks at the bottom?"

"Most likely."

"Bring it on," said Kuzco hopelessly as the limb tipped over the edge and plummeted down the falls.

The limb vanished in the towering mist at the bottom of the waterfall. Then a few seconds later it bobbed up. The vine that held them had loosened in the fall. Pacha struggled free and swam to the surface. But Kuzco was sinking. Pacha grabbed him in his strong arms and towed him to shore.

"Your Highness? Your Highness? Can you hear me?" Pacha tried. Kuzco lay motionless on the sand. "Oh boy, come on, breathe. BREATHE!" Pacha slapped

Kuzco's llama cheeks. He tried to pump the water out of his chest. Nothing. With a groan, the peasant realized he would have to try mouth-to-mouth resuscitation.

"Oh, why me?" he moaned. He took a deep breath, placed his lips on the yucky llama lips, and got ready to blow.

Kuzco's eyes flew open. Pacha opened his eyes at the same instant, and llama and peasant reeled away from each other, wiping their lips on their sleeves and spitting in disgust.

Exhausted from their ordeal, and stranded deep in the jungle, Pacha set up camp and started a small fire.

Unable to get over the idea that his royal lips had touched peasant lips, Kuzco washed himself and gargled with river water.

"For the last time, it was not a kiss," insisted Pacha.

"Whatever you call it . . . it was disgusting, and if you would have done what I ordered you to do in the first place, we all could've been spared your little 'Kiss of Life.'"

Kuzco spit out some of the water he'd been gargling and doused Pacha's fire with it.

"Aw," groaned Pacha in frustration.

"But now that you're here, you will take me to the palace. I'll have Yzma change me back, and then I'll start construction on Kuzcotopia. Oh yeah!" said the emperor.

Pacha could not believe the audacity of this llama. He walked away to calm his fury, took a deep breath, and turned back toward Kuzco. "Okay, now, I think we got off on the wrong foot here," he said diplomatically. "I just think that if you really thought about it, you'd decide to build your home on a different hilltop."

"And why should I do that?" Kuzco dried himself with Pacha's poncho and tossed it over the fire, putting it out once again.

Pacha restrained his anger. "Because, deep down, I think you'll realize that you're forcing an entire village out of their homes just for you."

Kuzco gazed at Pacha without sympathy. "And that's . . . bad?"

"Well, yeah! Nobody's *that* heartless."

"Hmmm." Kuzco pretended to ponder. "Now take me back."

"Wha . . .? Wait, wait! How can you be that way?" Pacha cried in total disbelief. "All you care about is building your summer home and filling it with stuff for you."

"Duh, yeah. I get everything I want because I'm the emperor. You're the only one who doesn't seem to be with the program, eh, Pacha?"

"You know what?" replied Pacha. "Someday you're going to wind up all alone, and you'll have no one to blame but yourself."

"Yeah, thanks. I'll log that away. Now, for the final time, I order you to take me back to the palace."

"Or what?" quipped Pacha. "Looks to me like you're stuck out here, because unless you change your mind, I'm not taking you back."

Pacha poked at his fire angrily, trying to get it started again. Kuzco made mocking motions behind his back and threw an acorn at his head. Pacha glared at him menacingly.

"Huh, what?" Kuzco acted indignant. "I didn't do anything. Somebody's throwing stuff. Are you going to build your fire or what?"

Pacha sighed. "He's never gonna change his mind," he said.

Night had fallen and there was not much farther either of them could go that day. Pacha settled down to sleep near the fire.

Kuzco sat some distance away, looking at the dark jungle around him. "How am I ever going to get out of here?" he wondered. He lay on the hard ground and tried to sleep. Soon the cold of the jungle night crept into his bones.

Pacha noticed Kuzco shivering. He laid his poncho over the emperor and returned to the fire. Kuzco looked up at the kind peasant, and wondered why the man was continuing to be nice to him. He just couldn't understand such behavior.

Chapter 7

The Wit and Wisdom of Kronk

The next morning Yzma draped herself in black and climbed to the pulpit of the royal cathedral to start Kuzco's funeral service. Hundreds of mourners shuffled into the pews carrying candles and singing the funeral dirge.

Everyone bowed their heads as Yzma began the eulogy. "And so it is with great sadness that we mourn the sudden departure of our beloved prince . . ."

Kronk sniffled and dabbed his eyes with a hankie. "Poor little guy."

". . . taken from us so tragically on the very eve of his eighteenth birthday. His legacy will live on in our hearts for all eternity."

She bowed her head. Then, as the music stopped, she took a quick breath and hurried to a conclusion: "Well, he ain't getting any deader!" She threw off her black veil to reveal a red sequined dress and feather boa. "Back to work!" she cried.

The mourners gaped at her for a second, then scattered away to fulfill their orders. On vases, statues, and banners all over the city, images of Kuzco were to be replaced with images of Yzma.

Yzma lounged on a high royal chaise while Kronk served her food. "Kronk, darling, I must admit you had me worried when you mixed up those poisons," she said sweetly. "But now that Kuzco is dead, all is forgiven."

"Oh, oh yeah, he's . . . he's dead all right," replied Kronk nervously. "I mean, you can't get much deader than the dead he is right now. That is, unless we killed him again."

"I suppose," said Yzma absently.

"Hey, look! The royal dresser is here!" said Kronk with exaggerated cheer.

As the dresser climbed a ladder to the chaise, Yzma turned to Kronk and knitted her brow in suspicion. "Kronk?"

He tried to ignore her. "I should tell you right now,

I'm kinda hard to fit. I wear sixty-six long with a thirty-one waist," he babbled to the dresser.

Yzma kicked the royal dresser off the platform. "Kuzco is dead, right? Tell me Kuzco is dead. I need to hear those words."

"Do you need to hear all those words exactly?" he asked.

Yzma dropped her plate of food and grabbed Kronk by the collar. "He's still alive?" she shouted.

"Well, he's not as dead as we would have hoped," said Kronk.

"Kronk!" Yzma gritted her teeth.

"Just thought I'd give you a heads-up, in case Kuzco ever came back," Kronk ventured.

"He can't come back!" she yelled.

"Yeah, that would be kinda awkward, especially after that lovely eulogy."

"You think?" Yzma retorted sarcastically. "You bumbling fool, you and I are going out to find him! If he talks, we're through. Now, let's move!"

Yzma decided to travel in comfort. She perched herself inside the royal litter—her exclusive traveling box—and Kronk strapped the litter on his broad shoulders. He traipsed from one village to the next, searching for Kuzco.

Yzma held a map of the jungle and made X's through all the villages surrounding the palace that they had searched. "Still no sign of Kuzco! Where is he?" she muttered. She grabbed the speaking tube that connected her through the window of the litter to Kronk's ear. "Kronk!" she shouted.

"Kronk here."

"I'm getting tired, pull over."

"Sure thing. Kronk out."

Kronk bent down, and Yzma climbed out of the litter, using his shoulders and arms as steps.

As she reached the ground her feet sank into the jungle mud. "Oh perfect!" she cried in disgust. "These are my best shoes!" She tossed her muddy feather boa over her shoulder angrily.

Kronk had spotted a pretty bird and was checking it off on his bird-watching bingo card. "Oh look, a golden-throated, small-winged warbler!"

Meanwhile, a swarm of bees went after Yzma. "Ugh! I hate this jungle!" she cried. She turned on them with a can of bug spray. "Get away, get away, get away . . ."

"I'm loving this," said Kronk with a sigh.

Yzma tripped and fell into the mud. Just then, Bucky the squirrel hopped out of the bushes. "Gu gug buh?" the squirrel asked, offering Yzma an acorn.

"Get away from me!" she cried.

Kronk couldn't help smiling at the cute little squirrel. Bucky leaped into his arms. "Whu guh guh buh guh!" Bucky cried, nodding in Yzma's direction.

"Yeah, tell me about it," said Kronk sympathetically.

"Guh gu buh guh?" Bucky asked.

"No, no it's not you. She's not the easiest person to get close to." Kronk pointed to his heart. "There's a wall there. Trust me."

"Are you *talking* to that squirrel?" asked Yzma.

"I was a Junior Chipmunk," replied Kronk. "I had to be versed in all of the woodland creatures."

Bucky and Kronk continued their chat.

Yzma rolled her eyes and stalked away. "Ugh, why me? Why me?"

"It doesn't always have to be about you," called Kronk. "This poor little guy's had it rough. Seems a talking llama gave him a hard time the other day."

Yzma stopped dead in her tracks. She spun back and eyed the squirrel. "Talking llama? Do tell."

Bucky whispered in Kronk's ear.

"Uh, he doesn't really want to talk to you," said Kronk.

"Well then, *you* ask him!" shouted Yzma.

Kronk sighed and muttered to himself. "Hate being

in the middle." He whispered the question to Bucky. Bucky whispered back, telling Kronk all about the rude llama and his narrow escape from the jaguars.

Yzma breathed down their necks, impatient to get her information.

Kronk gave Yzma a look. "Could you give us a little room here?"

"Oh, sorry," growled Yzma. She backed away.

"A little bit more, please," suggested Kronk.

Yzma stalked to the far side of the camp. Bucky relaxed a little.

"That's good," called Kronk.

"Now ask him which way the talking llama went!" shouted Yzma.

Chapter 8

Crocodile Lunch

That evening, just as Pacha's children had settled into bed, Yzma's faraway shout seemed to tear through Tipo's dream. "Dad! Look out!" he yelled.

His mother rushed to his bedside to comfort him. "Tipo, what is it?"

"I had a dream that Dad was tied to a log and going down a raging river!" he cried.

"All right, all right, it's okay," Chicha said soothingly.

"It was awful."

"Shhh, it's okay. Tipo, calm down. It was just a dream. Your dad's fine. He just went back to see the emperor," said Chicha.

"Oh," said Tipo, "like you told him to 'cause you're always right?"

"That's right," said Chicha.

Chaca sat up in her bunk. "Well, in my dream, Dad had to kiss a llama."

"Yeah, like that would ever happen," said Tipo.

"It could," said Chaca.

"Good night, you two . . ." sang Chicha.

The next morning, Pacha and the emperor woke up in the jungle, far from home. Pacha went to the riverbank and splashed water on his face. Kuzco walked down beside him.

He gently placed the poncho at Pacha's feet and thanked him.

Pacha looked up from the water. "Huh? Oh, no problem."

"Feels like wool," said Kuzco.

"Yeah," said Pacha.

"Alpaca?" asked Kuzco.

"Oh, yeah," said Pacha. "It is."

"I thought so," said Kuzco, stroking his own fur. "It's nice."

"My wife made it." Pacha smiled.

"Oh, she knits?"

"Crochets."

"Crochets . . . nice."

"Mmm. Thanks."

They stared at the river in silence.

"So, I was thinking that when I got back to the city, uh . . . we'd . . . uh . . . I mean, there's lots of hilltops, and maybe I might, you know, I . . . I might . . ." Kuzco seemed to be struggling with an uncharacteristically generous new idea.

Pacha stared at the emperor suspiciously. "Are you saying you've changed your mind?"

"Oh, well, I . . . uh . . ."

"Because you do know that means you're doing something nice for someone else," Pacha cautioned him.

"No, I know that. I know," said Kuzco.

"And you're all right with that?" asked Pacha.

"Yes!" Kuzco huffed, exasperated.

Pacha stared at the emperor. Was he serious? Pacha tried hard to read the expression on Kuzco's face.

"What?" Kuzco squirmed.

Ever the optimist, Pacha made up his mind. He thrust out his hand and offered to shake. "Don't shake unless you mean it," he said. Kuzco stuck out his hoof and they shook on it.

Pacha was elated. His beloved village would be saved! "All right!" he cheered. "Let's get you back to the palace."

After hours of jungle trekking, they finally emerged in a clearing on a hilltop. Pacha spotted the stone walls of the palace gleaming in the distance. He stopped and smiled in relief. Pacha showed Kuzco the welcome view.

"Okay," he said, "once we cross that bridge over the canyon, it's only an hour to the palace."

"Good," replied Kuzco, "because, believe it or not, I think I need a bath."

Pacha sniffed the air and raised his eyebrows. "I believe it," he muttered to himself as he started to cross the old bridge.

Suddenly the peasant's foot broke one of the bridge's floorboards. Then **SMASH!** A huge hole opened up and Pacha fell through. The ropes that had strung the bridge together caught around Pacha's waist, one of his arms, and an ankle. They held him suspended over the chasm. Dizzy from the fall, he saw crocodiles circling in the river far below.

Kuzco peered down at Pacha through the hole.

"Kuzco, quick!" cried Pacha. "Help me up!"

Kuzco stepped gingerly onto the bridge. "No," he said with a smirk. "I don't think I will." He hopped over the hole Pacha had made.

"You're gonna leave me here?" cried Pacha.

"Well, I was going to have you imprisoned for life,"

said Kuzco, "but I kinda like this better."

Pacha felt the ropes slowly giving way. "I thought you were a changed man," he said.

"Oh come on, I had to say something to get you to take me back to the city," said Kuzco.

"So all of that was a lie?" asked Pacha, the ropes cutting into his ankle and wrist.

"Well, yeah. No, wait . . ." Kuzco thought a bit, just to make sure. "Yeah. It was all a lie. Toodles!" he shouted, and began to walk away.

"But we shook hands on it!" bellowed Pacha.

Kuzco popped his head back down the hole and laughed. "The thing about shaking hands is . . ." He held up his hooves. "You need hands!"

Just as he turned to trot back over the bridge, more of the old floorboards gave way, and before he knew it, he was dangling over the chasm, side by side with Pacha. Down below, the crocodiles chomped their teeth in anticipation.

"Are you okay?" Pacha said with a gasp.

"Yeah, I think so," said Kuzco, dazed.

Pacha glared at the arrogant llama. "Good." He wound back his loose left arm and punched him in the jaw. "That's for going back on your promise!" he shouted.

Kuzco karate-kicked the peasant with his one free

leg. "That's for kidnapping me and taking me to your village, which I'm still going to destroy, by the way."

Pacha careened against the far wall of the canyon, then bounced back toward the infuriating llama. He held his fists straight out in front of him.

"No touchy!" cried Kuzco.

BLAM! Pacha sent Kuzco flying into the other wall of the canyon. The collision sent Pacha sailing back to the opposite wall. They clung to the crumbling rocks of the canyon walls, facing one another and still quarreling.

"Why did I risk my life for a selfish brat like you? I was always taught that there was some good in everyone, but oh, you proved me wrong," fumed Pacha.

"Oh, boo hoo," said Kuzco with a sneer. "Now I feel really bad. Bad llama."

"I could have let you die out in that jungle, and then all my problems would be over!" Pacha cried.

"Well, that makes you ugly *and* stupid," Kuzco jeered.

In a wild fury, they let go of the rock walls and swung toward each other again. Pacha held up his fists. Kuzco karate-kicked. As peasant and llama collided beneath the bridge, they heard the dry old structure begin to crack. Terrified, they stopped poking and punching each other and looked up over their heads.

CRRRAAACK! The bridge broke in the middle and sent them crashing together into one wall. The old ropes gave way, and Pacha and Kuzco tumbled against the rocks. They plummeted toward the hungry crocodiles.

Suddenly, the huge peasant and gangly llama found themselves wedged together in a narrow crevice. They looked down and panted in terror.

Kuzco panicked. "What are we going to do? We're going to die!"

"No we're not. Calm down," said Pacha. "I have an idea. Give me your arm. Okay, now the other one." Moving slowly, he showed Kuzco how they could link elbows behind them. "When I say 'go,' push your back against my back and we'll walk up the hill. Ready? Go!" Pacha pushed with his legs before Kuzco was ready and he smashed Kuzco against the rocks.

"You did that on purpose!" cried Kuzco. He pushed back, hard.

"No I didn't!" cried Pacha. "Now we're gonna have to work together to get out of this, so follow my lead. Ready? Right foot—"

"Whose right? Your right or mine?" asked Kuzco.

"I don't care . . . mine!" cried Pacha.

"Why yours?"

"Okay, *your* right. Ready?"

"Okay, got it."

Right, left, right, left. They stepped together, back to back, inching ever so slowly upward.

"Look, we're moving!" cried Kuzco in surprise. He glanced down into the dizzying chasm. "Aaaaaahhh!"

"Don't look down," said Pacha. "Now, stay with me. Right, left, right . . ."

As they moved higher, the gorge widened, and they were forced to stretch out their legs farther and farther until they could reach no more. They couldn't go another step.

"What now, genius?" asked Kuzco.

"Working on it!" Pacha declared.

Just above them, Pacha could see a tree branch with part of the rope bridge dangling from it. "Okay, here's the deal. Stretch out your neck, and I'll grab the rope."

"How do I know you won't let me fall after you grab the rope?" asked Kuzco.

"You're just gonna have to trust me," said Pacha.

With his head and neck, Kuzco pushed Pacha as close to the rope as he could. Still, it was just out of Pacha's reach.

"You know, it's a good thing you're not a big fat guy, or this would be really difficult," jeered Kuzco, pushing harder.

Pacha stretched out his arm as far as he could reach. "Ugh . . . almost . . . Got it!" He yanked the rope and it tightened around the branch. The tree shook, and scorpions rained down around them.

One crept onto Kuzco's stomach. As he screamed and batted it away in disgust, his hind hooves began to slip down the rock wall.

"Kuzco!" cried Pacha. In the nick of time he reached out with his free hand and grabbed Kuzco by the tail. The llama swung down like a pendulum, crashed into the canyon wall, and ended up with his head wedged in a cave. A flock of bats awoke and flew at his face.

"Aaaaahhh!" Kuzco leaped away, screaming. He scrambled up the wall, pulling Pacha along with him. Together they made it up to the canyon's rim and plopped down on the edge, speechless. They threw each other a glance and began laughing.

Suddenly the ledge began to rumble. The ground under Pacha was giving way!

"Look out!" cried Kuzco. He grabbed Pacha and pulled him to safety just as the ledge collapsed.

"Whoo, yeah! Look at me and my bad self! I snatched you right out of the air!" cried Kuzco, elated. He thumbed his llama nose at the canyon. "Ooh, I'm a crumbly canyon wall and I'm taking you with me. Well, not today, pal!" He did a dance of triumph along the canyon's rim.

Pacha stared at Kuzco. "You just saved my life."

Kuzco stopped in his tracks. "Huh? So?"

"I knew it," said Pacha.

"Knew what?" asked Kuzco.

"That there is good in you after all."

"Oh, no." Kuzco shook his llama head.

"Admit it."

"Uh-uh. Wrong."

"Yes, there is . . ."

"Nuh-uh."

"Hey!" cried Pacha. "You could have let me fall."

"Come on. What's the big deal? Nobody's that heartless," Kuzco said.

Then he gasped in disbelief that those words had actually just left his mouth.

Chapter 9

Table for Two

After nearly becoming food for the crocodiles, Pacha and Kuzco realized they were famished. Pacha steered them toward the jungle dwellers' favorite hangout for a bite to eat.

"Oh, hey, we're here!" cried Pacha as he glimpsed the diner's sign through the trees.

As they hurried to the door, they spotted a smaller sign that said: NO LLAMAS! No problem—they had gotten out of jams bigger than this one!

Quickly, Kuzco asked Pacha to give him his poncho and hat, and the llama dressed himself up to look like a woman.

They slipped into a booth, and Kuzco buried his face in a menu.

The waitress arrived to take their order. "Welcome to Mudka's Meat Hut, home of the Mug . . ."

Kuzco lowered the menu and batted his eyes at her. He fluffed his wig. The waitress stared at him for a moment, speechless.

" . . . of Meat," she managed to finish. "What'll it be?"

"Ahem. We'll have two specials," said Pacha. He made goo-goo eyes at Kuzco. "Is that all right, dear?"

"Oh, whatever you say, pumpkin, you know what I like," Kuzco gushed.

Pacha giggled nervously at the waitress. "We're on our honeymoon."

"Bless you for coming out in public." She grabbed their menus. "So, that's two specials."

"And an onion log . . ." Kuzco gave Pacha a mushy look. "To split."

The waitress went to the counter and called to the chef: "I need two heartburns and a deep-fried doorstop on table twelve!"

Pacha and Kuzco doubled over with laughter.

"Okay, so I'll admit this was a good idea," said Pacha.

"When will you learn that all my ideas are good ideas?" asked Kuzco.

Pacha rubbed his chin thoughtfully. "Well, that's funny, because I thought that you going into the jungle by yourself, being chased by jaguars, and lying to me so I'd take you back to the palace were all really *bad* ideas."

"Oh, yeah, anything sounds bad when you say it with that attitude," said Kuzco.

Just then the waitress returned. "Hot and crispy pill bugs for the happy couple," she said. "*Mazel tov.*" She tossed a handful of confetti on them without enthusiasm and turned back to the kitchen.

Pacha tapped the top of the bug and it opened up, letting off a burst of steam. "Oh boy!" he cried.

Kuzco looked on in disgust as Pacha slurped the bug through a straw. He slid out of the booth.

"Where are you going?" asked Pacha.

"I'm just gonna slip into the kitchen and have a word with the chef," said Kuzco.

"You're gonna get us thrown out," warned Pacha.

"Oh please," Kuzco said, primping his wig. "With this disguise, I'm invisible."

Pacha was busy sipping his bug and worrying about Kuzco, when Yzma and Kronk came through the door.

Exhausted, Yzma slumped in the booth behind Pacha's, complaining, "We've been walking around in circles for who knows how long. That is the last time we take directions from a squirrel. I should have done away with Kuzco myself when I had the chance."

Overhearing that last sentence, Pacha nearly choked.

"Aw, you've really gotta stop beating yourself up about that," Kronk told her.

Yzma growled at him in fury. Instead of wringing his neck as she wanted to, she grabbed her fork and twisted it out of shape.

"Uh-oh, I'll get you another one there, Yzma." Always the helpful assistant, Kronk turned and tapped Pacha on the shoulder.

Pacha grimaced. How was he going to get out of this?

"You using that fork, pal?" asked Kronk.

Pacha handed it to him over his shoulder without a word.

Kronk studied Pacha's profile. "Hey, don't I know you?"

"I don't think so," said Pacha.

"Wrestled you in high school?" guessed Kronk. "Metal shop? Oh I got it—Mrs. Nardka's interpretative dance class?"

Pacha stood and smiled politely. "Uh, no, look, I don't think we've ever met, but, uh, look, I gotta go." He slipped away and headed toward the kitchen in search of Kuzco.

"Don't worry, I'll think of it," Kronk called after him.

Pacha poked his head through the swinging kitchen doors.

Kuzco was busy annoying the chef. "Look, all I know is, the food looked iffy, all right? And I'm not the only one who thinks that, I'm sure."

"Psssst." Pacha tried to get Kuzco's attention.

"So I'm just checking to make sure you're gonna take the main course up a notch," Kuzco rattled on.

Over in their booth, Yzma was asking Kronk if there was anything on the menu that was not swimming in gravy.

"I'll go ask the chef," said Kronk.

By then the poor chef was about to explode. Kuzco went on with his attack. "It's a simple question: is there, or is there not, anything edible on this menu?"

Pacha glanced back into the dining room only to find Kronk headed toward the kitchen. He threw himself upon Kuzco and shoved him into the pantry just as Kronk swung through the door.

"Hey, I didn't ask him about dessert yet," complained Kuzco.

In the kitchen Kronk was asking the chef if he made special orders. Already infuriated by Kuzco's nagging, the chef threw down his hat. "All right, buster, that's it! You want a special order, you make it! I quit!"

"Is this really the best you could do?" Kuzco says, refusing to pick a bride.

It's Ignore the Pleas of the Peasants Day for Yzma and her assistant, Kronk.

Yzma and Kronk pick a potion to get rid of Kuzco . . .

. . . but it turns him into a llama!

Pacha refuses to help Kuzco unless the emperor/llama stops
his plan to build a summer home on top of Pacha's village.

"Whoa!" Kuzco meets some killer jaguars in the jungle.

"You call this a rescue?" Kuzco sputters to Pacha. "Well, I don't see *you* coming up with any better ideas!" Pacha retorts.

Bucky the squirrel tells Kronk and Yzma all about the rude llama he met—the very llama they are looking for!

"No touchy!" Pacha and Kuzco try to settle their differences high above a chasm with hungry crocodiles waiting below.

"Look out!" Kuzco cries, actually helping someone else for the first time ever.

Lunchtime at Mudka's Meat Hut.

Yzma pretends to be Pacha's long-lost third cousin's brother's wife's step-niece's great-aunt twice removed.

Tipo and Chaca cheer as Yzma goes flying!

"It has to be one of these!" Kuzco and Pacha search for the potion that will make Kuzco human again.

The wrong potions turn Kuzco into a lizard, a cow, an octopus, a bird, a turtle—even a whale!

Kuzco finds something he can really treasure—good friends who love him.

Kronk wondered what he had done. He had seen sensitive chefs before, but none this touchy.

"You know I try and I try and . . ." the chef muttered to himself.

"Hold on." Kronk tried to calm the chef, but he wouldn't hear it.

". . . and there's just no respect for anyone with vision! That's it! There's nothing I can do about it!"

Kronk panicked. "Wait a second! Please don't go!" he begged.

"Good day!" said the chef as he stormed out the back door.

Just then the waitress stuck her head in the pickup window to shout an order. "Three pork combos, extra bacon on the side . . ."

Kronk realized she was talking to him. "Yeah, but I—" he began to explain.

" . . . two chili cheese samplers, a basket of liver and onion rings, a catch of the day, and a steak cut in the shape of a trout."

For a moment Kronk stood there, stunned.

"You got all that, honey?" asked the waitress.

"Three oinkers wearing pants, a plate of hot air, a basket of Grandma's breakfast, and change the bull to a gill. Got it," repeated Kronk like a pro.

Inside the pantry Kuzco tried to struggle free from Pacha's grip. "What's going on?" he demanded.

"There's no time to explain. We gotta get out of here!" cried Pacha. He opened up a window and tried to push the emperor outside.

"In a minute, I'm still hungry," said Kuzco.

"No, Kuzco!" Pacha whispered urgently.

While Kronk was under the kitchen counter rummaging around for a pot, Kuzco waltzed back in. "Okay, I'll make it simple for you," he said. "I'll have a spinach omelette with wheat toast. Got it?"

"Can do," replied Kronk.

Before Kronk could look up, Kuzco had headed for the dining room. Pacha dashed out of the pantry to catch him. But just as Kuzco swung out the OUT door, Yzma, who was wondering what on earth was taking Kronk so long in the kitchen, was swinging in through the IN door. Pacha hid under a cabinet.

"Kronk, what are you doing?" asked Yzma.

"Kinda busy here," replied Kronk. He fumbled under the counter for a bowl. Pacha handed him one.

"Yo! Order's up!" Kronk shouted to the waitress.

Yzma decided to go with the flow. "All right, while you're at it, make me the special."

"Check! Pick up!" Kronk cried.

As Yzma went back out the OUT door, Kuzco came back in the IN door. "On second thought, make my omelette a meat pie," he said.

Kuzco popped OUT. Yzma popped back IN to change her order.

Then she popped OUT, and Kuzco popped back IN to change his order once again!

In and out they went, changing their orders over and over until the patient Kronk finally blew up. "Aw come on, make up your mind!" he cried.

"Okay, okay, on second thought . . ." said Kuzco.

". . . make my potatoes a salad," he and Yzma said together.

For an instant they were both in the kitchen at the same time. Yzma glanced over to where she thought she'd heard the familiar voice, but Kuzco had vanished. She jiggled her finger in her ear, thinking she must be hearing things.

Yzma went back to her seat. Kuzco had already returned to his and was studying his menu.

Pacha finally crept out of the kitchen, just in time to see Kuzco sitting in his booth with only the menu preventing Yzma from identifying him. Pacha knew he had to create a diversion. He called the waitress over and whispered in her ear.

"No problem, hon," replied the waitress.

Yzma had just spied Pacha's oddly dressed "wife" over the menu. She was leaning forward, squinting and trying to get a better look, when all of a sudden a crowd of waiters and waitresses gathered around her and shouted, "SURPRISE!" She felt a big birthday hat being plunked on her head, and before she knew it she was being serenaded by the waiters and waitresses.

Befuddled, Kronk peered out of the kitchen. "It's your birthday?"

In the midst of the confusion, Pacha grabbed Kuzco and ran. Once outside, Kuzco struggled to break away from the peasant's grip. Pacha held him in a headlock.

"What are you doing?" cried Kuzco.

"There're two people in there looking for you!" cried Pacha.

"What?"

"A big guy and a skinny old woman!"

"Wait," said Kuzco. "Was this woman scary beyond all reason?"

"Oh yeah!" replied Pacha.

Kuzco brightened. "That's Yzma and Kronk! I'm saved!"

"Trust me, they're not here to save you!" declared Pacha.

"They'll take me back to the palace," Kuzco murmured to himself. "Thanks for your help, you've been great. I can take it from here," he told Pacha.

"No, no, you don't understand! They're trying to kill you!" warned Pacha.

"Kill me?" Kuzco laughed. "Their whole world revolves around me!"

Pacha tried to hold the egotistical emperor back. "No, I can't let you—"

"What, what? Oh, oh, I get it. You don't want to take me back to the palace. You want to keep me stranded out here forever," said Kuzco.

"No!" the peasant protested.

"This has all been an act. And I almost fell for it."

"Will you just listen to me?" pleaded Pacha.

"No," fumed Kuzco, "you just listen to me. All you care about is your stupid hilltop."

"What?" Pacha couldn't believe his ears.

"You don't care about me. Now, just get outta here! Go!" shouted Kuzco. He spun away from the peasant and ran off.

"Fine!" called Pacha. He'd had enough of that spoiled brat of an emperor anyway.

Meanwhile, Yzma stormed out of the restaurant, blaming Kronk for all the confusion.

"What'd I do?" asked Kronk innocently.

Kuzco trotted up behind them, and was soon close enough to overhear their conversation.

"If you hadn't mixed up those poisons, Kuzco would be dead now!" he heard Yzma growl. "There will be no more diversions until we track that llama down and kill him!"

Kuzco ducked out of sight and kept listening. Pacha had been right! Why hadn't he listened to his friend?

"I said I was sorry," Kronk whined to Yzma. "Can't you let it go, even on your birthday?"

"Kuzco must be eliminated," Yzma declared. "The empire will finally be rid of that useless slug."

"Well, you've got a point," agreed Kronk. "No one really seems to care that he's gone."

Stunned, Kuzco watched Yzma climb into the royal litter. As Kronk carried her off, Kuzco raced back to where he had left Pacha. But the peasant was nowhere to be found.

"Pacha?" Kuzco cried. But there was no one there to help him. Dejected and with nowhere left to go, he wandered aimlessly through the jungle. He came to a clearing where he could see the palace and the royal city in the distance, and he tossed down Pacha's poncho and hat. At that, the skies darkened and it began to pour. Kuzco lay down in the rain alone.

Chapter 10

Get That Llama!

In the middle of the night the rain clouds blew away, and the stars began to shine brightly over the jungle trees. Kronk sat up in his tent. His foggy brain seemed to have cleared up with the sky. "The peasant!" he exclaimed. "At the diner!"

He struggled to hold on to his thought. "He didn't pay his check." And there was something else . . . something he couldn't quite remember. He lay down again and began to drift back to sleep. Then suddenly, it hit him! He bolted upright. "It's the peasant who I saw leaving the city who disappeared into the crowd with Kuzco on the back of his cart!" he cried. "He must've taken him back to his village—so if we find the village, we find him, and if we find him, WE FIND KUZCO! Oh yeah, it's all coming together."

Kuzco flung back the flap of Yzma's tent. Once he'd gotten over the frightening sight of her in a mud mask with cucumber slices on her eyes, he tried to explain. They must find Pacha's village! *That's* where they would find Kuzco!

The next morning, Kuzco awoke and started wandering again. In a nearby valley, he found a herd of llamas grazing. He was hungry and homeless and he was, after all, a llama now, so he decided to try to graze along with them. "Yech!" he cried as he gulped down his first bite of grass and steeled himself for another. Maybe he would get used to it.

He was munching and munching and feeling pretty sorry for himself, when from the midst of the herd he thought he heard a familiar voice. He hid behind the other llamas and listened.

"So there we were, standing on the cliff, and the ground started to rumble," he heard the voice say. "And just as it started to go, he grabbed me before I fell! Do you believe that?"

Kuzco moved closer to the voice. The llamas started to clear away, and there he saw Pacha—sitting on the ground, talking to the animals! "I know there's some good in him," he was saying. "Besides, I couldn't just leave him out here all alone."

Kuzco stood there and stared, dumbfounded.

"He's a lousy llama. I mean a really . . ." Pacha looked up and spotted Kuzco. ". . . lousy llama." He smiled.

"Listen. You know what I said to you . . . back at the diner? I, I . . ." Kuzco stammered.

Pacha held up his hand. He didn't need any apologies. "So, you tired of being a llama?" he asked.

"Yes!" cried Kuzco, his eyes wide.

They dashed toward Pacha's village. "Okay, we're just gonna stop at the house and get some supplies," said Pacha.

"And then we'll be on our way, right?" asked Kuzco.

"Right," said Pacha.

As they went up the hill, they passed a couple of old men playing checkers. "Hey there, Pacha!" called one of them. "You know, you just missed your relatives."

"My relatives?" asked Pacha, baffled.

"Yeah," agreed the other. "We just sent them up to your house."

"What did they look like?" asked Pacha, afraid to find out.

"Well, there was this big guy and this older woman

who was—how would you describe her?" the first old man asked the other.

"Scary beyond all reason," the other replied.

"Yeah, that's it."

Pacha and Kuzco exchanged a horrified glance. What were they going to do? Yzma and Kronk had arrived already!

In fact, at that very moment Chicha was pouring tea for them and trying to figure out where these two strange people, who claimed to be her husband's long lost relatives, had come from.

"So, remind me again on how you're related to Pacha?" Chicha asked.

"Why, I'm his third cousin's brother's wife's step-niece's great-aunt—twice removed," clarified Yzma.

She leaned back casually and looked at Kronk. "Isn't that right, Kronk?"

Kronk was too busy playing jump rope with Tipo and Chaca to reply.

Chicha could see that something was amiss, and she decided to hurry these two strange characters away. "You know, I am so sorry that you had to come all of this way, but as I said to you before, you may recall, Pacha is not here. I'll be sure to tell him you came by." She handed Yzma her coat.

"Oh, would you please?" Yzma oozed. "That would

be just . . . great." With that she purposely spilled her tea on the floor. "Oops, silly me!"

While the pregnant Chicha bent over slowly to clean up the spill, Yzma dashed over to Kronk and whispered, "She's hiding something! When I give the word, we search the house." Then she backflipped soundlessly back to her chair before Chicha was able to stand up.

"So, while we're waiting for Pacha, perhaps we could have a tour of your lovely home," Yzma weaseled.

"Why don't you just come back when Pacha gets home," said Chicha. "I'm sure he'd love to show you . . ." She hesitated. She spotted Pacha in the window, and he was trying to tell her something!

"Kitchen," he mouthed silently, pointing in that direction.

"Er . . . excuse me, I think I left something in the oven," she told Yzma, smiling apologetically.

Pacha met her and explained everything. He was telling her how he and Kuzco had to get back to the palace and find the right potion in the secret lab so they could turn him back into a human, when Kuzco popped his llama face in the kitchen window.

"Hi," he said.

Startled, Chicha clocked him on the head with her frying pan.

"Uh, that was him," said Pacha.

"Oh, sorry," said Chicha. "Go, go! I'll stall them long enough for you two to get a head start."

"Thanks, honey!" he cried. He kissed her.

Kuzco lifted his head, dazed. "Thanks, honey," he echoed.

As the two of them fled, Kuzco asked, "Are you sure it was a good idea to leave your family with those two?"

Pacha knew his wife well. "Oh, don't worry," he said. "They can handle themselves."

While Chicha was in the kitchen, Yzma had been trying to ransack the house for clues, but Tipo was pestering her and wouldn't leave her alone. Suddenly Chicha strolled back in and poured on the hospitality. "So, where were we?" she asked enthusiastically.

"Listen, sister," growled Yzma, "we're not leaving until—"

"I show you the house, of course!" Chicha finished her sentence.

Sometimes there were definitely advantages to having a run-down old house. As Yzma and Kronk toured one of her large closets, Chicha grabbed the loose door handle and pulled it off. Tipo slammed the door shut, and their houseguests were left in the dark. "The door's stuck!" Yzma yelled, clamoring to get out.

"What do you mean the door's stuck?" Chicha asked innocently. "Try jiggling the handle."

"There is no handle in here!" Yzma shouted.

"There's not? Are you sure?" asked Chicha. The kids giggled, seeing the handle in their mother's hand.

"All right, I've had enough of this!" cried Yzma. "Tell us where the talking llama is and we'll burn your house to the ground!"

"Uh, I think you mean *or*," corrected Kronk.

"Tell us where the talking llama is OR we'll burn your house to the ground!" cried Yzma.

Chaca peered through the keyhole. "Well, which is it? That seems like a pretty crucial conjunction."

"Ugh! That's it! Kronk, break the door down!" Yzma shouted.

"Break it down?" questioned Kronk. "Are you kidding me? This is hand-carved mahogany!"

"I don't care, you fool!" stormed Yzma. "Out of my way. I'll break it down myself!

"A one, a two . . ." Yzma got ready.

"Kids, you know what to do," said Chicha.

"Right, Mom!" Tipo and Chaca said.

". . . a three!" shouted Yzma. She ran full-tilt toward the door.

Calmly, Chicha opened the door and Yzma burst out. Her feet hit the floor, which Tipo had just polished, and she slid out of control toward the front door. Chaca opened the bottom half of the door and, **WHAM!** Yzma flew, feet first, out the door, sailed through the air, and landed in a wheelbarrow.

As the wheelbarrow bumped down the hill, Tipo splashed Yzma with honey from his beehive. Chaca opened up a pillow and covered her in feathers.

Just Yzma's luck, the wheelbarrow carried her smack into the middle of a birthday party, where the blind-folded children mistook her for a piñata.

WHACK, WHACK, WHACK. They hit her enthusiastically with their sticks.

"Ow! Ouch! Stop it, you little brats!" she cried. Pushing the feathers away from her eyes and fending off the blows, she spotted footprints along the road. She looked up, and on the horizon she saw Pacha and that infuriating llama!

"There they go, Kronk!" she yelled. "They're getting away. Kronk!"

At the front door, Kronk was handing Chicha a little notecard with his name and address on it. "I had a great time," he told her. "Let's not wait until the next family reunion to get together."

Chicha just smiled.

"Kronk!" shouted Yzma again.

Kronk glanced fondly at the children. "I . . . I gotta run."

Chapter 11

Showdown at the Schnozz

Pacha and Kuzco raced through the jungle. They had to make it back to the palace before Yzma did, or else Kuzco would be spending the rest of his miserable life as a llama! They dashed through an open field, then skidded to a stop at the edge of a cliff. Without missing a beat, Pacha pulled out his bow and arrow and shot a rope across the chasm. He slid on the rope over the deep valley, and Kuzco followed.

When they had reached the other side, they saw Kronk running toward the cliff, with Yzma leaning out the window of the royal litter. Quickly, Kuzco gnawed through the rope with his llama teeth and it fell free.

As Kronk approached the cliff, he picked up speed. Yzma put on her flying goggles. Kronk made a gigantic leap and pulled a lever on the litter. *WHOOSH!* A pair of wings popped out of the sides, and they went soaring across the valley. All was going well when, *KA-POW!* A bolt of lightning came down from a rain cloud and knocked them out of the sky!

Meanwhile, Pacha and Kuzco made it back to the palace. They stood inside, trying to figure out how to get into Yzma's lab. Pacha pulled the wrong lever for the secret door, just as Kronk had done before. A drenched Kuzco emerged from the deep well with a crocodile on his tail.

"Okay, why does she even have that lever?" he asked, kicking the crocodile away.

Pacha pulled the other lever, and the secret door slid open. They leaped into the roller-coaster car and whooshed down.

Together they searched Yzma's lab for the right potion. "What does it look like?" asked Pacha.

"I don't know. Just keep looking!" cried Kuzco frantically.

Pacha discovered Yzma's cabinet full of vials. "Over here!" he cried.

"It has to be one of these," said Pacha, reading the labels. The one labeled "humans" seemed to be missing!

Suddenly a voice stopped them cold. "Looking for this?" It was Yzma! She was holding the exact potion Kuzco needed.

Kuzco was in shock. "No, it can't be! How'd you get back here before us?"

Yzma flashed a questioning glance at Kronk. "How did we?"

Kronk scratched his head and studied the map. "Why, you got me. By all accounts it doesn't make sense."

"Oh well," quipped Yzma, "back to business."

"Okay, I admit it, maybe I wasn't as nice as I should've been, but, Yzma, do you really want to kill me?" asked Kuzco.

"Just think of it as, 'you're being let go, that your life's going in a different direction, that your body's part of a permanent outplacement,'" she jeered.

"Hey, that's kinda like what he said to you when you got fired," said Kronk dimly.

"I know. It's called a cruel irony. Like my dependence on you," said Yzma.

"I can't believe this is happening," said Kuzco.

"Then I bet you weren't expecting *this*!" Yzma pulled

a long knife from under her skirt and tossed it to Kronk. "Finish them off!" she ordered.

Kronk hesitated. His angel and devil voices were arguing once again.

"KRONK!" yelled Yzma.

Still he hesitated.

"Why did I think you could do this?" Yzma fumed. "This one simple thing! It's like I'm talking to a monkey!"

Ouch. Even Kronk's devil voice was offended now!

"And do you want to know something else?" Yzma continued. "I've never liked your spinach puffs!"

Kronk gasped. His angel and devil voices gasped, too! Tears welled up in Kronk's eyes. This was the last straw! The three of them looked up at the chandelier above Yzma's head.

"That'll work," Kronk decided. His angel and devil agreed. With one slash of the knife, he cut the rope holding up the chandelier, and it came clattering down toward Yzma.

But the center ring of the chandelier passed around her stick-thin body, and there she stood, unharmed and angrier than ever.

"Strange, that usually works," said Kronk.

"And so does this!" cried Yzma. She pulled a lever

and a trapdoor opened up under him, sending him plummeting down a long chute.

While Yzma had her eyes on Kronk, Pacha snuck up behind her and grabbed the vial.

"Ow! Give me that vial!" demanded Yzma.

They wrestled, and the vial slipped out of Pacha's hands. He dove for it, catching it just before it smashed to the ground. Yzma plowed into him and made a grab for it. Then Kuzco rammed her with his llama head and sent her careening into the vial cabinet.

The vial flew from Yzma's hand, while dozens of similar vials began to fall from the shelves and confuse the situation. "Oops, clumsy me!" she gloated. Now Kuzco and Pacha would never find the right one!

"Better hurry," she warned. "I'm expecting company."

An army of guards rushed in, ready to carry out her slightest command.

"Kill them! They murdered the emperor!" she ordered.

The guards shouted and prepared to charge.

"No wait! I'm the emperor! It's me, Kuzco!" the emperor pleaded. But the guards saw only a llama and a plump peasant.

"They're not listening to me!" cried Kuzco.

Pacha scooped up as many vials as he could and put them in his poncho.

The guards were rushing toward them!

Pacha tossed a bunch of vials at them. One hit the lead guard and he turned into a lizard. Another turned into a cow! Another became an ostrich, and yet another an octopus!

Yzma saw Pacha and Kuzco escaping in the chaos. "Get them!" she shouted angrily to the guards.

Pacha and Kuzco raced down a flight of stairs. "We've gotta change you back!" cried Pacha. "Try this one!" He threw the llama a vial.

POOF! When the pink smoke cleared, a small turtle sat on the stone floor.

"Uh . . . Pacha?" squeaked Kuzco. High over his turtle head, he could see the guards bearing down on him.

Pacha whisked his friend out from under the guards' feet and dashed away. He balanced Kuzco, with his hard turtle shell, on the banister, climbed on his back, and together they surfed down. Guards were behind them. Guards were down below in front of them.

Pacha chose another vial. "Oh, please be something with wings," he groaned. He poured the liquid into Kuzco's mouth.

POOF! Kuzco felt himself changing into a bird. "Yeah, we're flying!" he cried happily.

Kuzco flapped his wings. But his bird head was gigantic and his wings were way too small. He veered out of control. "Uh-oh," said Kuzco as he slammed into a wall.

"We're not getting anywhere with you picking the vials," Kuzco complained. "I'm picking the next one."

"Fine by me!" cried Pacha.

Peasant and bird started to cross a bridge over a canal. Kuzco grabbed another vial as they ran.

POOF! Suddenly he was huge. He covered the entire bridge. Kuzco had turned into a whale!

"Don't say a word," Kuzco said testily.

The bridge crumbled under his weight, and they plummeted into the canal.

"Quick, drain the canals," shouted Yzma as she raced up behind them.

Down below, Pacha and Kuzco surfaced. Pacha pulled out another vial.

"Open up," he told Kuzco.

Kuzco opened his enormous whale mouth and Pacha tossed the entire vial in.

POOF! Kuzco was a llama once more.

"Oh, yay," said Kuzco. "I'm a llama again." Suddenly the canal water began pouring out of the great palace. Carried out by the water, Pacha and Kuzco clung to the palace face to keep from being washed away.

Yzma peered down the palace walls. "Where did they go? After them!" she shouted to her guards. At her command, they jumped down the drain.

"Aaaaaahhhhhh!" they cried, flying right past Pacha and Kuzco.

Yzma growled at their stupidity. She found a long tapestry, and swung herself down.

Pacha and Kuzco climbed up to a ledge and rested, panting. Pacha looked at the vials. "Only two left. It's gotta be one of these."

WHAM! Completing her Tarzan swing, Yzma karate-kicked Pacha, sending the last of the vials flying. Kuzco dove to try and catch them. Yzma dove for them too. **CRASH!** They collided, head to head, and Yzma fell onto one of the vials.

"Nooo," groaned Pacha.

POOF! Yzma turned into a cat. She tried for a ferocious lion's roar. But all she could say was a tiny, squeaky "meow."

Kuzco and Pacha laughed and grabbed the last

vial from her seemingly harmless little paw. "This is the one. This'll change you back into a human," declared Pacha.

Kuzco was trying to pull the cork out of the vial, when the wild Yzma-cat sprang onto his head and began clawing him. "Ow! Get her off!" he cried.

Pacha tried, but she raked her claws at him, and he lost his balance.

"Whoa!" Pacha fell, catching himself on a small stone ledge. He hung by his fingernails, high over the hard pavement below.

Above him, Kuzco wrestled furiously with Yzma and pushed her away.

"Drink the potion!" Pacha cried.

Kuzco went to lift the vial to his llama lips, but it had vanished from his hoof.

"Looking for this?" Yzma yowled.

"No! No! Don't drop it!" cried Kuzco.

"I'm not going to drop it, you fool," meowed Yzma. "I'm going to drink it. And once I turn back into my beautiful self, I'm going to kill you!"

She tugged at the cork, but it wouldn't budge. She yanked and pulled and shook and banged the vial. But still the cork would not come out. Furious, she tried bouncing the vial on the ledge. It rolled over the edge, and she leaped to catch it. Somewhere in midair, she realized what she'd done.

"Aaaahhhh!" she cried, plummeting toward the pavement.

As the vial bounced down from ledge to ledge, Kuzco chased after it.

Pacha glanced down at the pavement and began to sweat. One by one his fingers began to slip. "Kuzco!" he cried.

The vial came to rest on a ledge. Kuzco looked at it. It was almost within reach! He glanced back at Pacha. "Be right there, just give me a minute."

Kuzco stretched for the vial.

"Kuzco!" Pacha was hanging by his pinkie!

The vial was so close, Kuzco could almost feel it in his hoof.

"Aaaaaahhhh!" Pacha fell.

In the nick of time, Kuzco did the right thing and swooped over to grab Pacha. As he pulled Pacha up to the ledge, they saw the vial teetering.

"The vial!" cried Pacha. It tumbled off the edge, catching up with the Yzma-cat, who was still falling.

Down below, a palace guard was quarreling with a delivery person. "For the last time, we did not order a giant trampoline," they heard the guard say.

Pacha and Kuzco stared in disbelief as Yzma and the vial hit the trampoline and bounced right back up.

Yzma spotted the vial flying up alongside her. She grabbed it in midair. She was laughing gleefully, when, SMACK, she crashed into the underside of a ledge and lost her grip on the vial. It bumped down the face of the palace and stopped on a narrow ledge. The vial wobbled and tipped.

"The vial!" cried Pacha. He glanced at Kuzco. "You thinking what I'm thinking?"

Peasant and llama once again linked hands back to back and climbed. They inched up toward the vial.

Yzma shook herself and leaped down toward the vial. It was just out of her reach.

Pacha strained toward it. He couldn't reach it, either! With his head and neck, Kuzco pushed the peasant closer. He did it! Pacha caught the vial in his hand.

But he held it for only an instant, when Yzma swiped at him with her paw and clawed it away. "I WIN!" she laughed maniacally.

WHAM! At that moment a door opened up out of nowhere and flattened Yzma against the wall.

Kronk poked his head out. "Whoa!" he said.

The vial fell out of Yzma's paw, and Pacha was right there to catch it. "Got it," he said, as he pulled Kuzco up to safety. Peasant and llama hugged briefly and then backed off, embarrassed.

"What are the odds of that trapdoor leading me out here?" Kronk said.

"Here, uh, let me get this for you," said Pacha, flustered. He popped out the cork and handed the vial to Kuzco.

Kuzco lifted the vial in a toast to his friend. "Well, see you on the other side."

"Meow," said Yzma.

Chapter 12

Kuzcotopia!

Back at home in the palace, the human Kuzco started getting into a new groove.

It was time to issue some apologies. First on his list was the old man his guard had thrown out the window.

"Oh you, stop being so hard on yourself. All is forgiven," the man said.

"Okay buddy," said Kuzco, "take care." He smiled to himself. "Sweet guy."

Then Kuzco caught a glimpse of someone sitting in the model room. He backed up and poked his head in.

It was Pacha sitting alone near the model of Kuzcotopia.

Kuzco went up to him. "So, you lied to me."

Pacha looked up. "I did?"

"Yeah," said Kuzco. "You said that when the sun hits this ridge just right, these hills sing. Well, pal, I was dragged all over those hills and I did *not* hear any singing."

Pacha smiled.

"So, I'll be building my summer home on a more 'magical' hill, thank you," Kuzco continued. He moved the Kuzcotopia model to the side.

Pacha handed the emperor the model of his own little house. "Couldn't pull the wool over your eyes, huh?"

Kuzco set Pacha's house back on the hillside where it belonged.

"No, no, I'm sharp. I'm on it. Looks like you and your family are stuck on the tuneless hilltop forever, pal."

"You know, I'm pretty sure I heard some singing on the hill next to us. In case you're interested," offered Pacha.

Kuzco looked at Kuzcotopia and rubbed his chin thoughtfully. He liked his new friend's idea.

That summer, Kuzco had a somewhat smaller, not quite so obnoxious home built just one hill over from Pacha's. Everyone's favorite part was playing in the river with the lovely rock waterslide.

"Ha! Boom baby!" shouted Kuzco as he kicked open

his door and emerged into the summer sun in his swim trunks.

"Ha! Boom baby!" echoed Pacha.

Kuzco zoomed down the waterslide and splashed into the water. Pacha swung over on a jungle vine. The big peasant did a cannonball and sent Kuzco flying to shore on a tidal wave.

There on the beach, Chicha was busy crocheting a new poncho for Kuzco. Kuzco stopped to admire her work.

Meanwhile, Kronk and Bucky were teaching the kids how to speak squirrel, translating such important phrases as "My acorn is missing!" and "Did you eat my acorn?"

It was a happy time in the kindgom for all!

Relive the Fun and Adventure with the Movie Soundtrack!

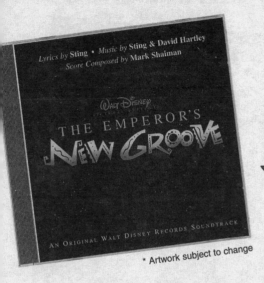

Lyrics by **Sting** • Music by **Sting & David Hartley**
Score Composed by **Mark Shaiman**

WALT DISNEY

THE EMPEROR'S
NEW GROOVE

AN ORIGINAL WALT DISNEY RECORDS SOUNDTRACK

* Artwork subject to change

Features lyrics by Sting,
music by Sting and David Hartley,
score by Marc Shaiman.
Performances by Sting, Tom Jones,
and Eartha Kitt.

Available wherever music is sold.